We Have to Get Rid of these Puppies!

We Have to Get Rid of these Puppies!

by *Marilyn D. Anderson*
illustrated by Bill Robison

Published by Willowisp Press, Inc.
401 E. Wilson Bridge Road, Worthington, Ohio 43085

Copyright ©1986 by Willowisp Press, Inc.

Printed in the United States of America

10 9 8 7 6 5 4 3 2 1

ISBN 0-87406-150-4

One

IF Mitzi had wanted to drive my whole family crazy, she couldn't have done a better job of it. Her timing was incredible. We had just moved to New York City, and we were still in shock at how small our apartment was. Lori and I were miserable in our new school. And tonight was New Year's Eve. We thought things couldn't get any worse, but Mitzi had other ideas.

Maybe I'd better explain that Mitzi is a dog. She's a lovable black mutt with hair all over. We've had her since I was six. Lori is my kid sister, and she's eight. She's also a pain, but I'll tell you more about that later.

Anyway, it was just after midnight when I

awoke. Dad was carrying me to bed. It felt so good that I let him go on thinking I was asleep.

Mom went down the hall ahead of us to open the door to the room I shared with Lori. She went over to the bed to turn down the covers. Then she stopped.

"Mitzi," I heard her whisper. "Get off!"

I smiled to myself and waited. The dog knows better than to get on the furniture, but she always seems to forget. When she gets caught, she usually acts very embarrassed. Then she wiggles away, trying to convince us she's sorry.

"Mitzi," Mom said again, louder this time. "Bad dog, get off the bed."

I opened one eye in time to see our usually sweet pooch growl and show her teeth.

That snapped me into action. Twisting myself free of Dad's arms, I dropped to the floor and reached for the dog. "Mitzi," I said. "What's the matter?" She didn't growl this time. Instead she moved away and groaned.

I glanced back at my parents. "She must be

sick," I wailed. "She's never acted like this before."

They were bending over the bed by this time, and nodding in agreement. "Maybe we ought to call Doctor Thomas," Dad suggested.

Mom looked thoughtful. "Something's wrong," she agreed. "But I hate to call a vet out on New Year's Eve."

I reached for Mitzi again only to touch something sticky. It was bright red. "She's bleeding!" I gasped.

Mom and Dad sucked in their breath and gave each other worrried looks. Just then, Lori squeezed between them, yawning and rubbing her eyes. "What's going on?" mumbled the shrimp. "How am I supposed to sleep with you guys making so much noise?"

"Why did she have to wake up?" I asked myself. Now we'll have to listen to Miss-Know-It-All tell us what's wrong and what to do about it. "Mitzi's sick," I said. "She's bleeding."

Lori stopped yawning and got interested. "Oh,

yeah?" she said, getting in for a closer look. "Where's it coming from?" I was about to tell her that I didn't know, when Lori's eyes grew wide. "Oh, wow," she yelled as she leaped into action. While the rest of us watched in amazement, she raced to her side of the room for paper and a pencil. Then she returned and flopped down at the foot of the bed. She began to write furiously.

I wanted to smack her. "What do you think you're doing?" I asked angrily. "Mitzi's sick and you're taking notes. Aren't you worried?"

Lori shrugged. "No, not really," she said. "But I am excited. It's not every day I see a batch of puppies being born."

The rest of us couldn't help laughing. "You're crazy," I scoffed. "You think Mitzi's having puppies? Whatever gave you that idea?"

"The movie I saw last week in school," she said without looking up.

"Oh, Lori," Mom protested. "Don't even think such a thing. What would we do with puppies?"

"Raise them, I guess," my sister answered. "I

wonder if Mitzi will have ten puppies like the dog in the movie?"

Dad sputtered and coughed. "Ten?" he croaked. "Did you say ten puppies? What a horrible thought."

"They were awfully cute," Lori assured him.

"I'm sure they were," said Mom. "But thank heaven Mitzi's a house dog. We don't need any more problems around here."

"They won't be any problem," Lori told her. "Look, the water bag is breaking."

The rest of us whirled around to see a flood suddenly appear upon my bed covers. "Oh, my gosh," said Mom.

"It can't be," Dad protested.

"It can't be, but it is," Mom realized. "George, do you remember when Mitzi disappeared for a few hours up at Grandma Bennett's?"

Dad held his head and nodded. "I'm afraid I do," he agreed. "But this is terrible. Do you think I should call Doctor Thomas after all?"

"Why?" Lori wanted to know. "She's not sick.

She's going to be all right!"

"Well, maybe he could give *me* something then," Dad moaned, "because I am. I can't stand to think of puppies in this apartment."

While all this was going on I'd been watching Mitzi carefully. She seemed to feel a little better for a while, but then she started to groan again. Her whole body strained. A big lump of stuff came out of her.

"There's the first puppy," Lori cried triumphantly. She checked my alarm clock and began to write. "He came at exactly 1:06 a.m."

I stared at the ugly mess on my bed with disgust. It sure didn't look like a puppy to me, but Mitzi seemed excited about it. She chewed her way through the gunk until a small black head appeared. Then she licked away some more. I could make out a teeny squashed-in nose and some floppy ears.

"Mom, Dad, we're grandparents," I marveled. They snorted a bit at that, but I could tell they were still upset.

"Only nine more to go," said Lori.

"Let's hope not," Dad groaned. "The supervisor of this building hates dogs. He'll want to throw us out if he ever hears about this."

"We don't have room for puppies here," Mom wailed. "How can she do this to us?"

"I don't know," my father answered. "But we'll have to give them away as soon as possible."

"Dad," I sputtered, "don't talk like that, especially not around Mitzi."

He rolled his eyes at me and continued in a whisper. "All right," he agreed. "I guess the dog doesn't have to hear about it yet, but you do. I want both of you girls to realize from the beginning that these puppies can't stay. Try not to get too attached to them."

I couldn't stand to think about it. Mitzi's family wasn't even all born yet, and already it was homeless.

Two

MITZI gave birth to three puppies in no time at all. She licked each one dry and made sure it got some milk. What a good little mother she was!

We waited a long time for something else to happen, but nothing did. Finally Dad said, "I think she's done, don't you?"

"Probably," Mom agreed. "And I think it's time we all got some sleep."

"But shouldn't we stay with Mitzi?" I asked.

"She'll be fine," Mom assured me. "What she needs right now is to be left alone."

Lori chewed on her pencil. "I should probably stay up and take some more notes," she said.

"No, you shouldn't," Mom told her firmly. "We're all leaving now, and the hall light goes out in fifteen minutes."

"Where am I going to sleep?" I wondered.

"You get the couch in the living room," Mom answered. She herded me to the door as she added, "Good night, Lori."

The next morning my sister was up early. "Kelly," she yelled in my ear. "Mitzi's puppies are gone!"

I burrowed deeper into the blanket and tried to ignore her. It's too early to face that smart aleck, I thought. But then I realized Lori had said something about puppies. It seemed as if I'd dreamed about puppies. . . .

"Kelly," she insisted as she pulled all the covers off of me. "Mitzi's in the kitchen eating like mad, but the puppies are gone!"

Suddenly, I was wide awake. I jumped to my feet and ran to our room with Lori on my heels. She was right. The puppies were not on my bed or anywhere else in the room.

"Where could they be?" Lori demanded.

"Maybe they're in the kitchen," I said. And I was off like a flash. We found Mitzi finishing the last of her food, but we didn't see any puppies.

"Mitzi," I cried, dropping to my knees. "Where are they? What have you done with your children?"

She looked at me innocently from under her dark bangs. What children? she seemed to say.

Lori grabbed Mitzi's head and put her face right next to it. "We want some answers here, Pooch," she insisted. "Where are those puppies?"

"Oh, Lori!" I said. "Ease up. She hasn't committed any crime. Let me talk to her."

My sister shrugged and moved aside. I patted Mitzi's head as she gave her dish a final lick. "Come on, Sweetie," I crooned. "You must be proud of your new babies. Let us see them."

But Mitzi wasn't listening so Lori and I sat back to consider things. "Maybe she hid the puppies on purpose," I said.

"Nah, why would she do that?" Lori scoffed.

"Maybe she heard Dad talking about giving them away," I said.

Lori rolled her eyes and looked pained. "That's a dumb thing to say," she told me. "Animals can't understand English."

"Maybe not," I admitted. "But sometimes they sense things you wouldn't expect them to."

"All right," she said, yawning. "Suppose you're right. What do you think we ought to do about it?"

"Wait," I said.

"Wait," she repeated. "For what?"

"For Mitzi to go back to her family," I explained. "Newborn animals have to eat all the time. That's something I learned in school."

My sister seemed doubtful, but she stayed to see what would happen next. Mitzi finished her breakfast with a long drink of water and wandered off. Lori and I trailed her right back to our room.

"The puppies aren't here, Mitzi," Lori said.

"Don't you remember where you left them?"

"Shhh," I said. "Just be quiet and watch."

Mitzi went right to my bed and jumped up on it. Then she began to poke around under my pillow which was pushed up against the wall.

"What's she doing?" my sister wanted to know.

"Shhh," I said.

We soon had our answer. A little black nose appeared from under my pillow and a furry little body followed. Then another puppy wriggled over to suck at Mitzi's side.

Lori and I went over to the bed. "One, two," I said, stroking the soft fur of the first pair lightly.

"Three," said Lori as she lifted the pillow to reveal a third puppy. "Hey," she added immediately. "There's another one here!"

I yanked the pillow out of her hands, and threw it on the floor. Surprise! There was a fourth black puppy. He was smaller than the rest, and he was trying to find his mother. Since his eyes were still closed, he wasn't having much luck. All he could do was wave his head from side to side and cry.

"Hi, there, little guy," I said, touching his nose with my finger. "Where did you come from?"

He stopped crying then and tried to suck my hand. When he raised his head, I could see a white bib between his front legs. "Hey, breakfast is over here," I told him.

His body was like a feather in my hand as I moved him into position at Mitzi's side. It must be rough to be that helpless, I thought. I don't envy him having to compete with three other puppies. I have enough trouble with one sister.

But the puppy didn't waste time feeling sorry for himself. As soon as he realized where he was he started sucking. That's when I decided he was my favorite, and I decided on a name for him.

"We'll call you Surprise," I told him so softly that Lori couldn't hear. "You're going to be a very special little dog, and we're not going to give you away."

Three

MY parents were amazed when they saw Surprise. "Where did he come from?" Mom wondered. "I thought three puppies were plenty."

"So did I," said Dad. "But I guess every litter needs a runt."

"He's not a runt," I protested. "He's just smaller than the others."

"And slower about getting here," said Dad. "Runts are always born last."

"Always?" Lori challenged.

"Sure," he teased. "Just look at what happened in this family."

"Dad," Lori complained, "that's not funny."

Mom put her hands on both their shoulders. "I hate to interrupt this high-level discussion," she said, "but we do have some important decisions to make this morning."

"Like naming the puppies?" I asked.

"No," she said. "I want to know where we're going to put these guys."

"My bed *is* a mess," I observed.

"If only we had a basement or a garage like we did in Vermont," Mom continued.

"Or a yard," Dad added.

"Or some friends," I said.

"We gave up a lot to move here," Dad concluded. "But I'm sure New York will grow on us."

"Like a fungus," Lori said doubtfully.

"Ahem," said Dad. "Back to the subject at hand."

"We don't have a good place for a litter of puppies," Mom complained. "And I'm worried sick about the carpeting."

"There isn't any carpet in the kitchen. The

puppies could live there," I said.

"Absolutely not," Mom answered quickly. "We'd be tripping over dogs all the time if they were in the kitchen."

"We could put them in a box," I said.

Dad snickered. "A box won't hold these guys for long," he said.

"How about the bathroom?" Lori suggested.

"The bathroom?" I sputtered. "Would you like to live in the bathroom?"

She shrugged and said, "I wouldn't mind if I had some good books."

"The bathroom is probably the only answer," Mom decided.

"I'll go see about a box right away," said Dad.

"I think I can find an old blanket to make everyone cozy," Mom added. And they were off to gather things for Mitzi's family.

It took Dad a long time to come back with his box. "I got it at the grocery store on Chestnut Avenue," he explained excitedly. "The store wasn't busy at all, so I had a nice visit with the manager. I was telling him how hard it's been for us to adjust to the city, and I happened to mention how much I like gardening. Well, he said he owned the lot next to his house, and that I'd be welcome to have a garden there. Isn't that great?"

Mom gave him a big hug. "Oh, honey," she said, "that would be wonderful. We could all help."

☆   ☆   ☆   ☆   ☆

The puppies didn't seem to mind staying in the bathroom at all. They burrowed right into their blanket and went to sleep. Mitzi, however, waited just long enough to get her family settled before jumping out of the box. She ran to the front door and whined.

Dad laughed. "Well, old girl," he said. "I guess you don't plan to be a homebody just because you've become a mother. Okay, just wait until I get your leash."

"That dog goes out more than I do," Mom said with a grin.

Dad looked at her over his glasses. "Is that so," he said. "And who was it who said she wanted to be a famous author? Who was it that insisted we have a typewriter in our bedroom?"

Mom shrugged. "I know what I said," she admitted. "And I love writing, but sometimes I get cabin fever."

"Then come for a walk with Mitzi and me," he urged.

She looked around the room hesitantly. "Well, why not?" she decided. "It's New Year's Day. What better way to celebrate? Do you girls want to come along?"

We shook our heads. "Somebody has to babysit the puppies," I said.

Later, Mitzi came bouncing into the apartment, smelling of fresh air. She ran straight for the bathroom. Lori and I were right behind her. Together we sat looking into the box.

"I wish we could play with them," I said.

"Hmmm," she answered with a shrug. "All they do is sleep. I can't think of anything else to write about them."

I looked over at her. "What did you want them to do, jump through hoops?" I challenged.

"Of course not," she said, "not yet anyway."

We were quiet for a while again. Then I said, "I like the smallest one the best. I even have a name for him."

"Like what?" she asked.

"Surprise," I said.

She wrinkled up her nose. "You mean, you won't tell me?" she asked.

I laughed. "I just did," I said. "His name is Surprise."

"What kind of name is that?" she hooted. "People will think you're crazy if you go around calling 'Surprise' and nothing happens."

"I don't care," I said stubbornly. "He surprised us by showing up late. It's the perfect name for him."

She sniffed. "Okay," she agreed. "If you call

the little one Surprise, I get to name the others."

"Well, maybe," I said. "But the names have to fit."

"No problem," she said. "We'll just call them A, B, and C."

"What?" I protested. "Your names are the ones that don't make any sense."

"Sure they do," she said importantly. "They're scientific names. I'm going to do an experiment with these puppies and win first prize at the science fair."

"Oh, yeah?" I said. "If you think you're going to starve any of these puppies so you can be a big shot . . ."

"Don't get excited," she said. "I'm not going to do anything like that. I just want to try a few of the things Pavlov did with his dogs."

"Pavlov who?" I demanded. "Is he some dumb kid at school?"

Lori snorted and said, "Boy, are you out of it. Pavlov was a Russian scientist who lived ages ago. He trained dogs to expect food when they heard a bell."

I got to my feet. "Well, listen to me, runt. I'm going to read up on this guy Pavlov, so you had better watch your step."

"I'm not a runt," she said fiercely.

Four

I had to go back to school a few days after the puppies came, and I dreaded it. Some of the girls had invited me to eat with them, but I still felt out of place. Luckily this particular day was a warm one so I took some paper and a pencil out to recess. I found a spot near the entrance to the building and sat down to work.

After a while I realized I was being watched. A pretty, dark-haired girl stood just behind me. Our eyes met, and she smiled.

"Hi," she said sheepishly. "I've been trying to figure out what you're doing."

I grinned back. "Thinking up names for dogs," I confessed. "Crazy, eh?"

She came closer. "Well, that depends," she said, "on whose dogs they are and why you're doing it."

I motioned for her to join me. "Our dog had puppies over vacation," I explained. "My sister wants to call them A, B, and C. I figured I'd better come up with some real names fast."

"A, B, and C?" she repeated. "Your sister sounds weird."

"How did you guess?" I giggled. "She drives me nuts."

"I have the same problem," said the girl. "Your name is Kelly, isn't it?" I nodded. "Mine's Sarah," she went on, "Sarah Miles."

"Okay, Sarah," I said, "what kind of names would you give our puppies?"

"I don't know," she answered. "Tell me about them."

"Sure," I said. "There are four, and they're all black. The mother is kind of a mutt but we think she's part poodle. No one knows what the father looks like."

"They sound cute," she decided. "I wish I could see them."

"Well, you can," I said, turning to face her. "Come home with me after school tomorrow. You'll get to meet all of them."

"Great," she agreed. "I'll ask my mother tonight."

I felt so good having talked with Sarah that I guess it showed. When I got home Mom seemed to sense something different about me. "How was school today?" she asked. "Did you get an *A* on that math test you were worried about?"

"Nope," I said, "but I think I made a friend. Can she come over after school tomorrow?"

Mom smiled at me and said, "Of course. I'll even bake chocolate chip cookies in her honor."

"All right!" I whooped.

"Lori, how was your day?" Mom went on. "Did you make any new friends?"

"Nah, the kids in my class are all dummies," she muttered.

The next day Sarah spent the whole lunch hour

with me. I found out that she had moved here just a few months before I had. She hated their apartment, too, so she spent a lot of time at the library. She promised to take me there soon.

By the time we arrived at my apartment after school, I felt I'd known Sarah forever. The minute she laid eyes on the puppies, she went bananas. She dropped to her knees by the box, and acted as if she wanted to crawl in with them. "Oh, I love them," she wailed. "Can I hold one?"

My father had said we could handle the puppies some, so I said, "Sure." Then I picked up Surprise and held her out to Sarah. "This one's my favorite," I said. "I named her Surprise because we were surprised to find her under the pillow. Now, she's just full of surprises."

Sarah laughed and gently took the puppy from me. "What a doll!" she crooned. "She fits right in my hands, and that white spot under her chin is so cute!"

"I know," I said proudly.

Sarah got well acquainted with Surprise before

she looked back into the box. "Oh, that one has wavy hair," she marveled. "Can I hold her?"

When I nodded, she handed Surprise to me and picked up the other puppy. "You should call this one Curly," Sarah said, rubbing the pup's soft fur against her chin. "It's a girl, isn't it?"

"Of course," I said. "And Curly sounds like a good name. Would you like to have her?"

"Would I ever," Sarah answered. "But my dumb sister is allergic to animals."

"Nuts," I said. "We have to give these puppies away. I know you'd have given her a good home."

About then Lori poked her head in the door. "What are you guys doing?" she asked.

"Nothing much," I told her.

She looked at us suspiciously. "Dad said we couldn't play with them, yet," she said. "I'm going to tell."

"We're not playing with them," I insisted. "Sarah's just looking them over."

Lori studied my new friend coldly. "Are you as silly about dogs as Kelly is?" she asked.

35

Sarah shrugged, and said, "I guess so. Are you Kelly's little sister?"

"Unfortunately, yes," she said. "I'm the brains in the family."

"Terrific," said Sarah.

"Yeah, that's terrific," I echoed. "Lori, why don't you go read a book or something. Sarah and I are busy."

"Might as well," she sneered. "You guys won't talk about anything interesting anyway."

When Lori had gone, I said, "That's a relief. Now we can get down to naming these puppies."

"Right," Sarah agreed. We returned Surprise and Curly to the box and studied the other two puppies carefully. Minutes later Sarah added, "I see what you mean about your sister. I'll bet she doesn't have many friends."

Five

EVEN though Lori drives me crazy most of the time, she is my sister. It sort of bothered me to have Sarah think my sister was weird.

"She acts differently down here than she did in Vermont," I said.

Sarah shrugged. "That's too bad," she said, "really too bad."

I nodded and changed the subject. "Now, about these puppies," I said. "We should probably give them names that start with A, B, and C. Then I won't have to argue with Lori."

"Good idea," Sarah agreed. "What do you think we should call that little monster?" she asked, pointing to a puppy chewing on Curly's tail.

I laughed. "He's a real troublemaker, isn't he," I said.

"We could call him Butch," she suggested. "That's a good name for a tough guy."

"I like it," I decided. "Now, what about the biggest one?"

"His name should start with an A," Sarah remembered. "Say, was he born first?"

"Yeah, I think so," I said. "Why?"

"Then, let's call him Adam," she said. "I think he needs sort of a dignified name."

"Okay," I agreed. "You have good ideas."

"Sometimes," she said, "but you had the best idea today."

"Which one was that?" I wondered.

"The one about me taking Curly," she said. "I'm going to work on my folks about that."

☆ ☆ ☆ ☆ ☆

As the puppies got bigger, they became more active. Their eyes were still closed, but they had no trouble finding their dinner these days. Mitzi seemed to think Lori and I were her own private babysitters. When we came in to see the puppies she would make sure we noticed her first. Then she would leave to find something else to do.

That was fine with me, because I loved holding Surprise. She would snuggle up next to me and lick my hands with her teeny weeny tongue. Lori pretended not to notice, but I think she was secretly jealous.

All my sister could talk about was her science project. She was determined to do a project using the puppies. That worried me because I'd read some scary things about her friend Pavlov. When I asked Lori for details, however, she only talked about having the puppies respond to a bell. She also planned to build a maze for them to run through and solve.

Mom bought Lori the bell she needed. It was one of those dome-shaped metal bells with a clapper that dings. Of course, Lori couldn't wait to try it. She charged into the bathroom, dinging away like mad, and Mitzi woke up with a start. When the dog saw who it was, she stretched, yawned, and lay back down. She continued to keep an eye on Lori, but the puppies slept through it all.

Lori tried again. This time she reached right into the box and rang the bell. Mitzi didn't appreciate that, and she stood up, growling.

I agreed with Mitzi. "Lori, cut it out," I demanded. I made a grab for the bell. "How would you like to have some jerk making a lot of noise when you were trying to sleep?"

"The puppies never heard me," she said, shaking her head. "They never even heard me."

Mom stuck her head in the door then and said, "Well, I heard you, and I want you to stop."

"I was just testing something I read," Lori explained. "The book said that puppies are not only blind at birth, but they're deaf, too. I just proved to myself that the book is right."

Mom sighed and moved on, but before she got out of earshot I heard her talking to herself. "That girl," she said. "I don't think I was cut out to be the mother of a scientist."

Mom and Dad decided that Lori would be allowed to ring her bell only once each day. They said that would be enough to check on the puppies' hearing. So every night at exactly seven o'clock Lori leaned over the box and gave one crisp ding. For about a week her only response was a look of disgust from Mitzi.

At last, the time came when Adam heard her. His head jerked to attention and he looked all around. You could see he was trying to figure out where the strange sound came from.

Lori got all excited. "He heard me," she announced to everyone within five blocks of our apartment. "Now, we're getting somewhere."

Mom and Dad hurried in to see what all the fuss was about. When Lori told them, Dad just shook his head. "And what does our junior scientist plan to do next?" he asked.

"I thought I'd teach the puppies to associate this bell with food. I plan to ring it whenever they start to nurse," she said. "Then, when I'm ready for the maze . . ."

"Wait a minute," Mom interrupted. "I think you've forgotten something."

Lori looked confused. "Well, the concept is scientifically sound," she said. "If you don't believe me, I can show you a place in our science book that explains . . ."

"That may be true," Mom said with a smile, "but how can you be here to ring the bell every time the puppies nurse? You have to go to school, you know. And Mitzi isn't going to notify you when she gives them their two o'clock feeding either."

Lori seemed crushed, but she brightened quickly. "I know," she said. "I could fix things up so that the bell rings whenever the puppies move around in the night."

The rest of us looked at each other hopelessly. "Listen, squirt," said Dad. "Even if you could find some way to ring the bell when these little guys nurse, I won't let you do it."

"Why?" Lori protested. "I have to do a science project, you know. And I want to win a prize."

"That's fine," said Dad. "But Mitzi's family deserves a little peace and quiet just like the rest of us."

I knew Lori would have to pout about that. She didn't disappoint me. "Humph," she grunted angrily. "You just don't understand." And she stomped out of the room.

When she had gone Mom looked at Dad and raised her eyebrows. "Sometimes I don't know what to make of that child," she said.

"I know what you mean," he said.

Six

LORI seemed to lose interest in Mitzi's family after that. She said she had a new idea for a science project. Soon our bedroom was filled with flowerpots of dirt. "They're bean plants," my sister informed me. "Beans are more reliable than dogs."

I wasn't impressed with her plants, but I loved watching the puppies. Their box was the first place I went after school. They had endless wrestling matches. Now that they could see and hear, they wanted to explore.

The first time I put Surprise on the floor she tried to waddle away, but she didn't get far. Her rubbery legs quickly collapsed and she plopped on the floor. I scooped her up for a hug, and we tried it again.

Sometimes I would lay on my side and let the pup try to crawl over me. No matter how hard she tried, she couldn't quite scale Mt. Kelly.

I guess I talked a lot about the puppies. When I did, Lori tried to show how bored she was. She'd say things like, "Wow, that's big news! We'd better call the paper," or "Does the President know about this?"

Sarah came over several times to play with Curly. She and I would sit on the bathroom floor, and use our legs as a fence around the puppies. Surprise was always determined to get out. She kept trying to climb over my legs long after Curly had given up.

One day we took all the puppies out of the box at the same time. That was a riot! They were determined to eat the shagged carpet. They pulled and pulled on the threads. I figured they couldn't do much damage yet, so I let them have their fun.

Butch soon decided my shoestrings were more interesting. He had them all untied before I could drive him away. Next he noted that Surprise was lying on her back and open to attack. Wagging his tail eagerly, Butch crouched down for a mighty charge. Surprise must have heard him coming because she leaped to safety in the nick of time. Butch lost his balance and slid into the rug, nose first. Sarah and I howled with laughter.

A few minutes later I realized we were missing a puppy. "Hey, where's Adam?" I asked, looking all around.

"The door's open," Sarah realized. "I thought we closed it."

"We did," I agreed. "Let's put these guys back and find Adam."

Our brave puppy hadn't gone far. He was in my parents' bedroom, barking furiously. We guessed he was afraid of the tassels on the bedspread.

As I scooped him up and turned, Lori suddenly appeared in the doorway. "Mom said the puppies had to stay in the bathroom," she teased. "I'm going to tell on you."

"Tattletale," I snapped. Then I had a brilliant thought. "You're the one who let him out," I said. "We had the door closed, but you just had to snoop, didn't you?" I saw by her face that my guess had been right.

"Maybe I did," she admitted. "I had to see what all the laughing was about."

"Then, I won't tell Mom, if you don't," I said. "Is it a deal?"

"It's a deal," she agreed.

A few days later I caught Lori in the bathroom holding Surprise. When she saw me, she put the puppy down immediately. "Just checking her reflexes," Lori announced. "She's all yours." I wanted to ask her which reflexes, but she made a fast getaway.

As the puppies got older I wanted to take them outside. Dad agreed they needed exercise, but he didn't want the building supervisor to see the puppies. He also insisted we find a place free of traffic.

I thought of the church parking lot a few blocks from our apartment. Except for Sundays, it was usually deserted, so we figured it ought to be safe enough. As we began to make our plans, my father told us that the whole family would have to help. I could hardly believe that Lori agreed without an argument.

On Saturday morning Dad handed each of us a grocery bag. He said we were each to keep a puppy out of sight until we were in the car. I wanted to take Surprise, but so did Lori. Naturally, she won as usual. So I got Curly, Mom took Adam, and Dad ended up with Butch.

None of the puppies liked going in the bags. Even Curly twisted and clawed as I lowered her into mine. "Come on, sweetie," I begged. "We're taking you to a nice place where you're going to have fun."

At last we were ready. Dad put Mitzi on her leash, and we started out the door. "I hope these guys keep their mouths shut," he said, pushing the "Down" button for the elevator. We all nodded, hoping the puppies would cooperate.

Two people were already on the elevator when it came, but we squeezed on anyway. An old lady who wore gobs of makeup eyed Mitzi uneasily. "Does it bite?" she wanted to know.

The other lady on the elevator was even older than the first, but she looked softer. Smiling kindly, she said, "Of course not. Can't you see this is a well-behaved animal?" Then she turned to Dad and asked, "May I pet her?"

Dad returned her smile and nodded. Then, just as the lady began to ruffle Mitzi's fur, I heard Butch whimper. He was loud and insistent. The old lady's ear was right next to his sack. She had to have heard him, but her expression never changed. Instead, she began to talk rather loudly to Mitzi. "Aren't you a good girl," she said. "Your family is very lucky to have such a good dog, aren't they?"

When Lori started to giggle, I stepped on her foot. Butch and the old lady kept going all the way to the main floor.

"Whew, that was close," I said, as we piled into the car.

"Can I take Surprise out of the bag now?" Lori asked.

Dad shook his head. "Let's not ask for trouble," he answered, and he drove to the very center of the church parking lot. We all looked around as if we were planning to break the law.

"There's only one car here," my father observed. "I don't think anyone will bother us. Everyone out."

We all carried our bags to the same spot and tried to remove the puppies. Curly didn't object, but the others had to be dumped out of their sacks. At first the whole crew just sat there, stunned by the size of the real world. Mitzi's motherly sniff seemed to spur the puppies into action. Soon they were running in all directions with my family running just as hard to keep up with them. We were much too busy to notice that we had company.

"Hello," said a strange voice. "Having fun?"

Seven

I whirled around, expecting the worst. Instead, I saw a friendly-looking man with a distinctive white collar showing above his topcoat.

"Sorry to startle you," he said. "I'm Pastor Schultz, and I saw your car drive up. When I saw what you were doing I had to come out."

The rest of us scurried to gather up the puppies while Dad offered the man his hand. "I'm George Bennett," said my father, "and this is my family. I hope you don't mind us taking over your parking lot."

"Not at all," the man assured us. "Your puppies are some real charmers."

We looked at each other and lowered the dogs

back to the asphalt. Butch immediately attacked the minister's pant leg, and the other three attacked Butch. As soon as Pastor Schultz freed his pant leg, Butch went after his shoestrings.

I was afraid the man would get angry. He just chuckled and shook his foot loose. "What's this one's name?" he asked.

"That's Butch," I said, embarrassed to death. "I'm afraid he has terrible manners."

"We live in an apartment on the third floor," Dad explained. "So these puppies have never been outside before."

About that time Adam took off. The others immediately galloped after him with their ears flapping. Lori and I managed to stay with the pack until a playful squabble slowed it down. Mitzi and the adults arrived minutes later.

"What a wild bunch!" the minister observed. "My kids would sure enjoy watching them. Butch looks like the kind of dog my son Barry would like. Do you plan to keep all these puppies?"

"I should say not!" Dad responded. "We need

to give them away as soon as possible."

"Well, the price is right," the man joked. "Now, if I can just convince my wife she needs a dog, we're in business."

"Do you think you might?" Mom asked eagerly.

The minister winked. "She's a soft touch," he said.

"Then, I'm sure you'll manage," my father chuckled. "Why don't I give you my phone number?"

When Pastor Schultz left, Dad returned to help us with the puppies. "That's one less dog to worry about," he said gleefully.

"Pastor Schultz is nice," I said. "But we don't know anything about his son."

Dad laughed and said, "Butch can take care of himself. I'd save my sympathy for the Schultz family."

The day had been such a success I decided to call Sarah and tell her about it. When I finished giving her the details, she said, "That sounds like fun. Why didn't you invite me?"

"It was a top secret operation," I told her. "Dad said the fewer people involved the better."

She giggled. "You guys were pretty cool," she agreed. "I'd have guessed you were carrying out garbage."

"Not if you heard Butch making all that noise," I said, laughing. "I can't believe Pastor Schultz likes him."

"Me either," she answered. "Not when he could have had Surprise or Curly."

"Speaking of Curly," I said, "have you talked to your parents about her, yet?"

She hesitated. "Yes, I've been bugging them like mad," she said with a sigh. "All they ever say is 'We'll see.'"

☆ ☆ ☆ ☆ ☆

Two days later the puppies escaped from their box and took over the bathroom. Mom groaned when she found the place redecorated with toilet paper and puddles. The second time it happened we began to put anything chewable out of reach. After that our whole life-style changed.

We had to stop taking showers because the shower curtain was in shreds. The bathroom floor was carpeted in three layers of newspaper, and it still smelled. When we took baths, the puppies tugged and chewed on the towels. I took Surprise in the tub with me once, but she didn't like it. She kept trying to crawl up my hair until we were both howling.

The day the puppies chewed a corner off the linen closet door, my mom hit the ceiling. "I can't stand this anymore," she exploded. "We have to get rid of these puppies!"

"They're not even eight weeks old," I protested.

"The books say we have to keep them until then," Lori agreed.

"The guy who wrote those books didn't have to live with a bathroom full of dogs," Dad pointed out.

"We just can't turn them loose, and we haven't

60

found people to take them yet," I said.

"Then get busy and find some," Mom said firmly. "The leftovers will have to go to the pound."

"Mother!" I gasped, "how can you even suggest such a thing?"

"Don't you care about Mitzi's family?" Lori sniffed.

"Of course I do," Mom said in a gentler tone. "But I also believe in being realistic. Our family can't survive much longer with five dogs."

"I'll find homes for the others," I promised. "You'll see."

Beginning that very day I asked everyone I saw about adopting a puppy. Most of them acted as if I had leprosy. My teacher rolled her eyes and shook her head violently. People on the street gave me strange looks and refused to answer. The other kids at school either had dogs or their building didn't allow pets. I was getting pretty discouraged until good old Sarah came through.

She called me one night, yelping with joy.

"Kelly, I've got terrific news!" she squealed. "My sister just decided to move out of the apartment and into a dormitory at college!"

I couldn't figure out what was so great about that so I didn't answer her.

"Kelly?" she wondered. "Are you there?"

"Yeah," I said.

"Well, aren't you glad?" she asked. I could tell she expected me to be.

"I don't know," I admitted. "Why?"

"Because this means a dog won't affect my sister's allergies. I can have Curly!" she shrieked.

"Oh," I yelled. "Oh, now I see! Oh, Sarah, thank you, thank you, thank you!"

She laughed and said, "Hey thank *you*. I'm the one who's getting a present."

My parents were almost as happy as I was when they heard the news. "Two down and two to go," Dad said. "Keep up the good work."

☆ ☆ ☆ ☆ ☆

That week something happened that my family will never forget. I was the first one home that night because Mom had taken Lori to the dentist. As soon as I stepped in the door, I knew something was wrong. I guess seeing the living room drapes half off their rods was my first clue. The puddles on the rug made things still clearer. The tissues and newspapers strewn all over and the half-eaten slipper in the middle of the floor were dead giveaways.

"The puppies are loose!" I wailed to no one in particular. "Heaven help us."

Eight

MITZI must have heard the door because she hurried toward me, whining an apology. I threw my coat on the nearest chair and raced down the hall, looking for the puppies. "What are they up to?" I asked myself as I followed the sound of breaking glass. They were in my bedroom.

"Lori's flowerpots!" I gasped, as the whole awful scene unfolded before my eyes.

Broken pottery, dirt, and tiny wisps of green were everywhere, with the puppies putting on the final touches. Butch and Adam were rolling in the mud from the plant roots, grinding it into the carpet. Curly was coyly chewing up the last recognizable bean plant. Surprise was playing with a pot that hadn't yet been smashed.

"Mom is going to have a fit when she sees this," I told the puppies. "Dad is going to scream and holler. And Lori will absolutely die. How could you do this?"

I saw that Mitzi had followed me. She knew I was angry. She hunkered down and rolled over on her back, wanting to be forgiven. But I was furious with her.

"Why didn't you stop these little monsters?" I demanded. "You're their mother." At that she got to her feet and slipped out the door.

Figuring I ought to catch the puppies and clean up the mess, I reached for Surprise. She must have thought I was playing because she darted under my bed with a mouthful of stems. She began to bark at me.

That got Adam's attention. Eyeing me suspiciously, he stood up and shook the mud from his coat. When I reached for him, he leaped away and barreled out the door. The other two puppies quickly made up their minds to follow him.

"Hey, come back here!" I screamed after them. "Don't go in the living room."

But that's exactly where they headed. I arrived just in time to see them dive under the couch. "Come out of there, you little brats," I fumed. And I looked around for something that might reach them. That's when I spotted Surprise coming to see what was happening.

"Good girl, nice puppy, hold still," I crooned as I inched toward her.

She rolled her eyes at me and stretched out her front legs. Her tail wagged mischievously. I almost had my hand on her when I felt a sharp prick on my ankle. I whirled around to see Butch disappearing into the kitchen. "Ouch," I bellowed. "That hurt." At the sound of my voice, Surprise stopped stretching and joined her brother. I caught sight of her tail disappearing behind the refrigerator.

About that time, the front door opened, and

Dad walked in. "Holy cow," he said in a shocked voice. "What happened here? I didn't know New York had hurricanes!"

"It's the puppies," I said. "They got out of the bathroom, and they're running wild."

"The building supervisor will sue us," he groaned. "We've got to catch them before they do any more damage."

"I've tried," I explained. "There're two under the couch and two behind the refrigerator."

"Get me a broom," he ordered, throwing his coat on the chair next to mine. "I'll show these guys who's boss."

"Good idea," I agreed and ran for the kitchen. I grabbed the first long handle I saw and raced back to Dad. "We need a plan," I said, handing him a dust mop.

"We need a broom," he said, looking at the mop. "I don't want to shake dust all over the house."

I nodded sheepishly and returned to the closet. When I came back, Dad said, "All right, here's the plan. I'll poke around under the couch and you catch the puppies when they come out."

"I'll try," I promised.

Curly panicked as soon as she saw the broom, and ran right to me. "Good work," said Dad. "We've got them now."

I stuffed Curly under my arm and prepared to grab her brother. Adam, however, managed to avoid the broom until it got to the very end of the couch. When he did come out, he ran between my father's legs and made for the kitchen. I never had a chance.

"Terrific," my Dad fumed. "Just terrific. Now we've got three behind the refrigerator."

While he plotted our next move, I took Curly down and locked her in the bathroom. Mitzi was already there, cowering behind the door. "Here," I said, "keep an eye on this one." And I slammed the door shut.

I found Dad on his knees next to the refrigerator with his right hand reaching as far as he could behind it. "I can't quite reach them," he muttered. He tried to back out of his position. He lost his balance and bumped his chin against the wall on the first try.

"I think I'm stuck," he gasped. "Kelly, come over here." So I got down by his left side and steadied him until he could pull his arm free. He stood up rubbing his arms and complaining.

"Well, let's try the broom again," he said at last. "But this time you do the poking. I'll do the catching."

"Okay," I agreed, and we each crouched down in our positions. I had just managed to work the broom between the wall and the refrigerator when the front door opened again.

It was my mother. She couldn't see us over the room divider. Her mouth dropped open and a terrible scream escaped. "We've been robbed!" she cried and pushed Lori back into the hall.

Dad and I forgot about the puppies and rushed after her. "Bernice, come back!" my father yelled. "It's not what you think."

She and Lori were almost to the elevator

before we caught them. "Come back," I panted. "There weren't any robbers. The puppies did it all."

My mother grabbed her head. "That's even worse," she cried. "I can't take it anymore."

As my father talked soothingly to her, I noticed that Lori was smiling. When she saw me looking at her, she brought her hand across her mouth. I had to do the same, because things suddenly seemed funny to me, too. We turned away to hide our grins, only to see real disaster in the making. The puppies had found the door to the apartment open. They were taking off down the hall!

"Dad, do something!" I shouted.

Nine

AS my family raced down the hall after the puppies, I heard loud talking behind us. "What is it?" "What's going on?" people were asking each other. "Call the super." "Yeah, the super should know about this."

But I didn't have time to worry about the people because the puppies had finally reached the end of the hall. They had nowhere else to run.

"We'll catch them now," Dad said confidently. "Spread out and get ready."

The puppies stopped at last and began to mill around. Butch immediately grabbed Adam by the neck, and Adam snapped back at him. As their fight got more intense, Surprise had to move fast to stay out of it. None of them were paying any attention to us. We would have nabbed the whole crew in seconds if a certain door hadn't opened just then. It was right next to the struggling puppies and offered a tempting escape route.

In a flash, Adam tore loose from Butch and dived through the door. Just as quickly, the door slammed shut again. The other pups' noses were nearly flattened as they tried to follow. Dad grabbed Butch, and Lori moved amazingly fast to pounce on Surprise. I tried to take the puppy from Lori, but she wouldn't let me. The chase was over, but our problems were just beginning.

"What are we going to do about Adam?" I asked.

"Let's forget we know him," Mom whispered.

The crowd was right behind us now. "Whose puppies are those?" "Where did they come from?" "How old are they?" "Can we pet them?" our neighbors wanted to know.

"I want a puppy, Mommy," a pint-sized girl wailed.

"We can't just leave Adam in that apartment," Dad whispered back. And his hand reached for the apartment's door bell.

Then, suddenly a stocky little man in a flaming red vest and a black bow tie came on the scene. His face was nearly as red as the vest. He was yelling at us as he came. I knew it had to be the building superintendent.

"What's going on here?" he demanded. "Are those dogs I see? Is that what all this uproar is about?"

"Well, yes, I'm afraid so . . ." my father began.

The man jumped on Dad's words before he could finish. "I remember you saying that you have one dog," the man fumed. "You plainly have two. What are you trying to pull here, Bennett?"

"Well, we didn't plan to have two dogs," Dad explained. "It just happened."

"I don't care how you got the second one," the man interrupted. "You broke the terms of your lease."

"But, sir," my father said desperately. "We're

planning to give the pups away."

The man's eyes bulged. "Pups?" he croaked. "Did you say pups? Does that mean you have the mother, too?" He started rummaging through his keys. "I want to see your apartment this instant," he went on, and he headed right for our door.

None of us wanted to be there when he saw the disaster area so we hung back in the hall. It was a good thing, too, because his yelling hurt my ears the way it was.

"Arrrrrrgh," he howled. "Look at this room! The drapes are ruined. The carpeting will never be the same. And what about the rest of the apartment? The bathroom, for instance. What have you done to it?"

"Oh, no," I cried as I ran to the apartment. The rest of my family panicked, too. We fell over each other getting through the door. We had barely slammed it shut behind us before Mitzi and Curly appeared. They rushed out barking joyously and proceeded to jump on everyone.

The superintendent returned to the living room

to view the doggie reunion. Hands on his hips, he glared at us as he said, "I don't believe it. Four dogs in one apartment? If you haven't disposed of the extras by tomorrow evening, I promise to have you evicted." And he stalked out the door.

I picked up Curly and held her close. "I sure wish Sarah could take both you and Surprise," I whispered to her.

The rest of the family didn't seem to know what to do. Dad and Lori, still holding their pups, just stood there watching Mom pace around the living room.

"Those drapes were pretty tacky before the puppies got to them," she said angrily. "And I think a good shampoo would fix the carpet. He's overreacting."

"I think so, too," said Dad. "This is the only room they touched. It could have been worse."

"Well, I'm afraid it is worse," I remembered.

Everyone looked at me. "What do you mean?" Dad asked.

I hated to tell him. "I mean, the puppies were in

our bedroom," I said.

Lori's eyes grew big with fear. "Our bedroom?" she cried, running from the room. "What about my plants?"

We found Lori on her knees amidst the remains of her experiment. Still holding Surprise, she stared at the awful mess for a moment and began to cry. As her crying grew louder, Surprise reached up and licked her face.

Mom put her hand on my sister's shoulder. "Oh, Lori," she said in a hushed voice. "Honey, I'm sorry. I know the plants meant a lot to you."

"It's not fair," my sister sobbed, and she stroked Surprise's damp fur. "I've got to win a ribbon. I've just got to."

Dad joined Mom at Lori's side. "We're all sorry about this," he said gently. "We know how hard you've worked and you deserve to win. But, Lori, winning isn't everything."

"It is, too," she insisted. "The kids in my class don't like you unless you're smart."

"I'm sure that's not true," said Mom. "And

besides, you are smart. We all know that."

"Then, why don't I have any friends?" Lori wailed. "I hate my school. I hate all the kids in it."

Mom put both arms around Lori then and held her tight. "Oh, honey," she said, "I'm sure you don't mean that."

Just then the doorbell rang. Dad got up to answer it.

Ten

THERE was nothing I could do to make Lori feel better, so I went with Dad to the door. Our caller was a familiar-looking lady who carried Adam in her arms. Suddenly, I realized she was the same person who had helped us with Butch in the elevator.

The woman smiled when she saw that Dad and I were carrying puppies, too. "Hello, I'm Mrs. Evans from down the hall," she said. "It looks as if I have the right apartment."

"I'm afraid so," Dad answered. "I'm George Bennett, and I'm very sorry about all the trouble we've caused you. Thank you for returning Adam."

"No trouble at all," Mrs. Evans assured him as she tickled the puppy under the chin. "I sort of enjoyed the excitement, but this poor fellow was pretty upset. I thought he should have a chance to calm down before I brought him back."

"I'm glad you waited," said Dad. "The building superintendent was ready to evict us for four dogs. He'd probably have shot us if he had seen five."

"Oh, you mean that man, Harold?" the lady chuckled. "Don't let him scare you. His bark is much worse than his bite."

"I wish I believed that," said Dad. "Please, come in and meet my family. This is my daughter, Kelly."

"Well, all right," the lady agreed, stepping through the door. "I'm glad to meet you both. I get terribly lonesome sometimes so you must come to visit me."

"Yes, ma'am, we will," I promised.

She surveyed our ruined living room with a twinkle in her eye. "I see your puppies had a

good time today," she said. "No wonder Harold was so cross."

Dad nodded. "He had a right to be angry," he agreed. "And we're ready to give the puppies away. It's just that we hate the thought of sending them to the pound."

Mrs. Evans stiffened. "The pound?" she protested. "How could you even consider such a thing?"

Dad shrugged. "The superintendent didn't leave us much choice. He insists we get rid of the puppies by tomorrow."

"Humph," the woman snorted as she held Adam tighter. "This is one puppy that isn't going to the pound. He's the nicest thing that has happened to me for a long time, and I want him. Is that all right with you?"

"Oh, that would be wonderful," I cheered. "Adam is the perfect dog for you."

About that time Mom and Lori came in to see who we were talking to. Lori had stopped crying, but I could tell by the way she hugged Surprise that she could start again at any minute.

Dad made more introductions and finished by saying, "And this lovely lady is going to take Adam off our hands."

Mom gave the woman a relieved grin. "Oh, good," she responded. "I knew you liked dogs that day we met you in the elevator."

The woman nodded and said, "They're really much nicer than the woman I was with that day. I swear, Grace never has a kind word for anyone. Sometimes I get so lonesome I'll even put up with her."

Mom did a double take. "I thought I was the only one crawling the walls around here," she said. "Maybe you and I could go shopping sometime. Do you like bookstores?"

Mrs. Evans's face lit up. "I adore them," she announced. "But I could never get Grace near one."

"Then it's all decided," said Mom. "How about tomorrow? No, you'd better make it next week. We've got to do something about the rest of these puppies tomorrow."

"Let's call Sarah," I said. "She can probably come for Curly in the morning."

"That's right," Dad agreed. "And Pastor Schultz seemed pretty positive about taking Butch."

"But what about Surprise?" I asked miserably.

Lori looked even more upset than I was. "Yeah, what about Surprise? You can't give her away. She's my friend."

"Why don't you just keep her?" asked Mrs. Evans.

"I doubt the superintendent would allow that," said Dad. "He's threatened to evict us."

Mrs. Evans snorted. "He wouldn't dare," she said confidently. "You see, I own this building."

"You what?" we all gasped.

"I said, I own it," she repeated. "Before my husband died, we had a big house in the suburbs. I couldn't stand to stay there alone, so I sold it and moved here. An apartment is really much more my size."

I began to hope. "Can we, Dad? Can we?" I begged.

"Yeah, Dad," Lori pleaded. "Please, let us keep Surprise."

But Dad shook his head. "You're very kind," he told Mrs. Evans. "But this apartment is really too small for a second dog."

"Then, we'll find you a bigger apartment," the woman decided. "A family on the ground floor is leaving at the end of the month. Their apartment has lots more room than this place. I'll let you have it for the same money."

"Well," Dad hesitated.

"We'll take it," Mom finished. "I'm dying to have my feet back on the ground again."

I was afraid Dad might still say no, but he didn't. "All right," he agreed. "I guess I'd like that, too."

I looked at Lori and she looked at me. We wiggled with joy. Now, if only Pastor Schultz would take Butch, everything would be perfect, I thought.

As soon as Mrs. Evans left, Dad dialed the minister's number. Lori and I kept our fingers crossed while they talked. When he began to smile, we cheered.

"He still wants Butch," Dad said, grinning broadly. "I don't know why, but he still does. He and his family will be over tonight to pick him up."

I spent the next few hours wondering what the minister's son would be like.

Eleven

BY the time the Schultz family arrived I had made up my mind that Barry would be awful. He was probably some snotty-nosed baby who liked to pull dogs' tails. Or maybe he'd read about Pavlov, too, and wanted to do terrible experiments on Butch. Thank heaven, I was dead wrong.

Barry turned out the be a year older than I am, and he was really nice. Although his dark eyes danced with mischief, he was gentle with Butch.

"Oh, Dad, he's super," the boy said, studying Butch's face. "I'll bet he's really smart, and I'll bet he learns to retrieve sticks just like Mike Haskins' dog."

"He's part poodle," I said. "Poodles make great retrievers."

Barry's mother and his sister Becky seemed nice, but for some reason Lori wouldn't talk to them.

Finally Mrs. Schultz cornered her and asked, "Lori, what school do you go to?"

"Jackson," she mumbled, pretending to read a magazine.

"Why, Becky, that's your school," the woman realized. "Do you two know each other?"

"Uh huh," Becky admitted. She gave a lot of attention to her finger which Butch was chewing on.

We all looked puzzled as my mom set out to settle the mystery. "Well, girls," she said. "If you know each other, why are you so quiet?"

"I wouldn't know what to talk about with her," Becky replied.

"Why is that?" Mrs. Schultz asked.

"Because she's a big brain," said Becky. "She's only interested in scientific stuff."

"Who told you that?" my mom wanted to know.

"She did," Becky insisted. "Some of the boys were teasing her when she first came. They called her a shrimp from the boonies. They said no one from Vermont knew anything. Lori told them she had gone to a school for geniuses. She thought everyone in our room was dumb."

"Lori," Mom sputtered, "did you really say that?"

"Yeah, I guess I did," she admitted. "Then I had to study like mad so they wouldn't find out how dumb I really was."

At that Becky finally looked directly at Lori. "You mean, you aren't a genius?" she asked. "Does that mean you like the same kind of things I do?"

Lori shrugged. "Maybe," she said. "What kind of things do you like?"

"Oh, lots of stuff," Becky said. "Like my Bootsie doll and all the clothes that she has."

Lori's eyes lit up. "I have Bootsie's pony," she

91

said eagerly. "Mine has a purple tail."

"Really?" Becky responded. "Mine has a pink one. Can I see yours?"

"Sure," Lori agreed. "Come on."

After they disappeared I found out that Barry liked to cheat at checkers. I still beat him two games out of three. Our parents spent the evening discussing kids. For some reason, they did a lot of laughing.

When we were alone again Dad sat down in his favorite chair and Mitzi wiggled her way on to his lap. "Well, you rascal," he said, stroking her contentedly, "you're full of surprises. This family has a lot of new friends because of your puppies, and that's good. But don't have any more!"

And she never did.

About the Author

MARILYN D. ANDERSON grew up on a dairy farm in Minnesota. Her love for animals and her twenty-plus years of training and showing horses are reflected in many of her books.

A former music teacher, Marilyn has taught band and choir for seventeen years. She specialized in percussion and violin. She stays busy training young horses, riding in dressage shows, working at a library, giving piano lessons, and, of course, writing books.

Marilyn and her husband live in Bedford, Indiana.